The Kissing Tree

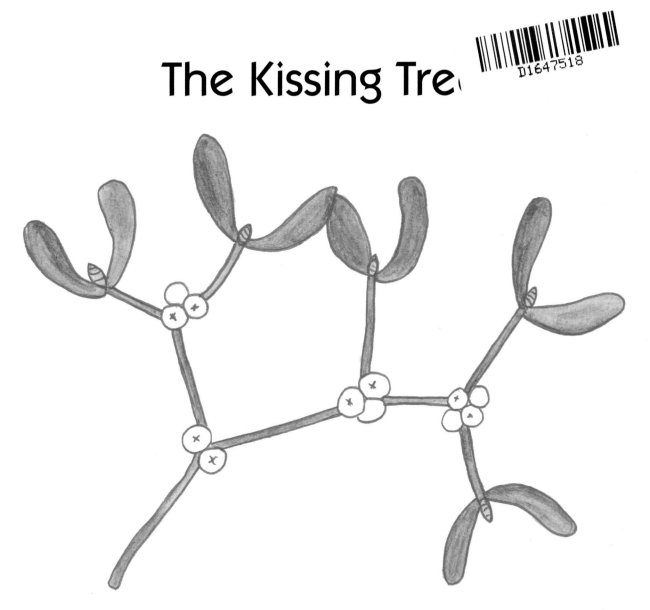

Helen Wendy Cooper

LANCASHIRE COUNTY LIBRARY

30118137212118

Lancashire Library Services	
30118137212118	
PETERS	JF
£5.99	10-Dec-2018
NLA	

Dedications

For Reg Farmer,
(Founder of Tenbury Mistletoe Association in 2004),
& Louisa Rose Bloy.
Helen Wendy Cooper.

http://www.fast-print.net/bookshop
The Kissing Tree
Copyright © Helen Wendy Cooper 2018

ISBN: 978-178456-579-4

All rights reserved
No part of this book may be reproduced in any form by photocopying
or any electronic or mechanical means, including information storage
or retrieval systems, without permission in writing from both the
copyright owner and the publisher of the book.

The right of Helen Wendy Cooper to be identified as the author of this work has
been asserted by her in accordance with the Copyright, Designs and
Patents Act 1988 and any subsequent amendments thereto.
A catalogue record for this book is available from the British Library

First published 2018 by
FASTPRINT PUBLISHING
Peterborough, England.

The Kissing Tree

A dark sleek bird flew down to a tree,
"What a splendid tree this is for me!"
He bounced from a twig, to a leaf, to a branch,
From the ground below it was a beautiful dance.

He grabbed some twigs and began his nest,
"I'll settle here," he said, "I'll have a rest."
"My name is Jack," he shouted out loud,
As underneath there'd formed a crowd.

Slugs, ants and bees came to see,
The dancing bird that was so happy!
"I'm a Jackdaw and I'd love a mate,
So if you see a lady Jackdaw, that'd be great!

I'll spread my scent and poo up this tree,
Then mistletoe will grow, so beautiful, you'll see!
My lady love will come and I'll be,
The happiest Jackdaw in this kissing tree!"

As days, weeks and months went on by,
Sweet berries grew that could be seen from the sky.
The Jackdaw smiled, so proud of his creation,
He loved to sing and tell the whole nation.

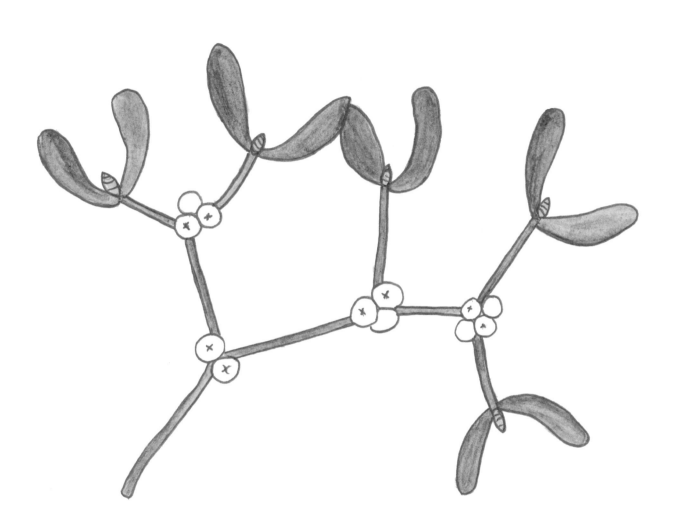

"Come and try some of my delicious mistletoe,
Fly up from the ground, ready, steady, go!
Come on bees, slugs, birds and ants,
Eat a berry, join in my merry dance!"

Later that day it grew cold and dark,
The Jackdaw closed his eyes; he'd begun to lose heart.
Why hadn't his lady love Jackdaw come?
Could she not see all the effort he'd done?

Sleep came to him as he lay in his nest,
And during this time he had an unexpected guest.
A Robin flew up to the Jackdaw's tree,
And ate every single berry it could see.

As morning light rose the Jackdaw awoke,
His voice so hoarse, he could barely croak.
"My mistletoe, my berries, where've they all gone?"
Oh no, someone's been here, what have they done!"

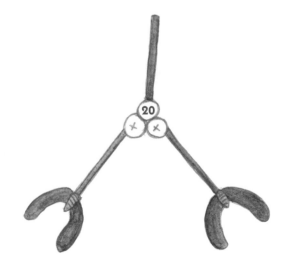

He flew around, his legs like a jelly,
Then at last he found one very last berry!
For hours he perched on a branch below,
Then finally the flames in his heart were aglow.

A beautiful bird flew through the sky,
Her wings so graceful, she soared so high.
A female Jackdaw, he could hear her sing,
He began to dance, he spread out his wing.

He sang his song and pointed his beak above,
The Jackdaw saw it, she was ready for love.
She landed by Jack and grabbed the berry,
Then sat in the nest feeling ever so merry.

She placed the berry safely on the tree,
Jack sat next to her so full of glee.
She pushed Jack the berry, she'd give it a miss,
They rubbed beaks together, a perfect mistletoe kiss!

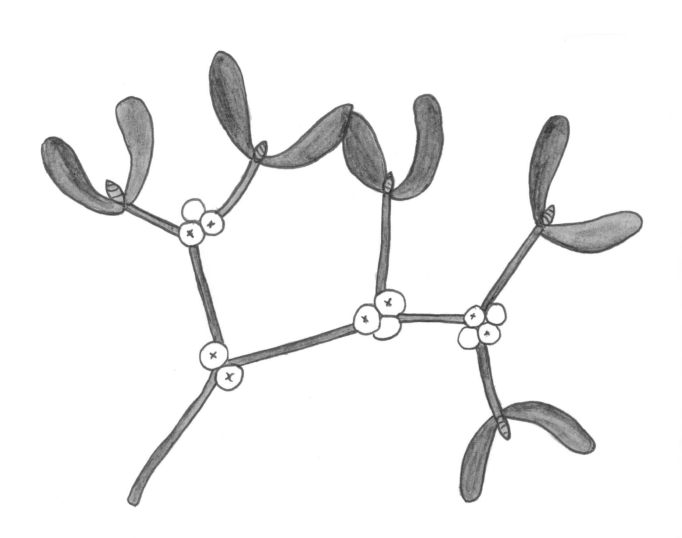

A few mistletoe facts…

o   There are around 1300 mistletoe species worldwide.

o   Mistletoe comes from the old Anglo-Saxon words mistle and tan, meaning poo on a stick.

o   Mistletoe can only grow on trees.

o   Lots of wildlife, including insects and birds, love to eat mistletoe, but the berries are not safe for people to eat.

o   People love to kiss under the mistletoe.

A special thank you to Tenbury Mistletoe Association in Tenbury Wells, the UK capital of Mistletoe! Without their knowledge and inspiring enthusiasm, I would never have thought to write The Kissing Tree.

Helen Wendy Cooper.

About the Author

Helen Wendy Cooper lives in Worcestershire with her fiancé, Andy, and daughter Louisa, two cats, two tortoises and some fish!

She loves animals and birds, so was delighted to be asked to write The Kissing Tree for Tenbury Mistletoe Association.

Helen's the author and illustrator of Rudy the Reindeer, The Vegetarian Vampire series and SHAPE LAND, which is a picture book series for under-fives.

She was also a judge for CITV Share a Story 2017 and BBC Radio 2's 500 words 2018. She absolutely loves reading children's stories and hopes children enjoy her books too!

www.helenwendycooper.co.uk